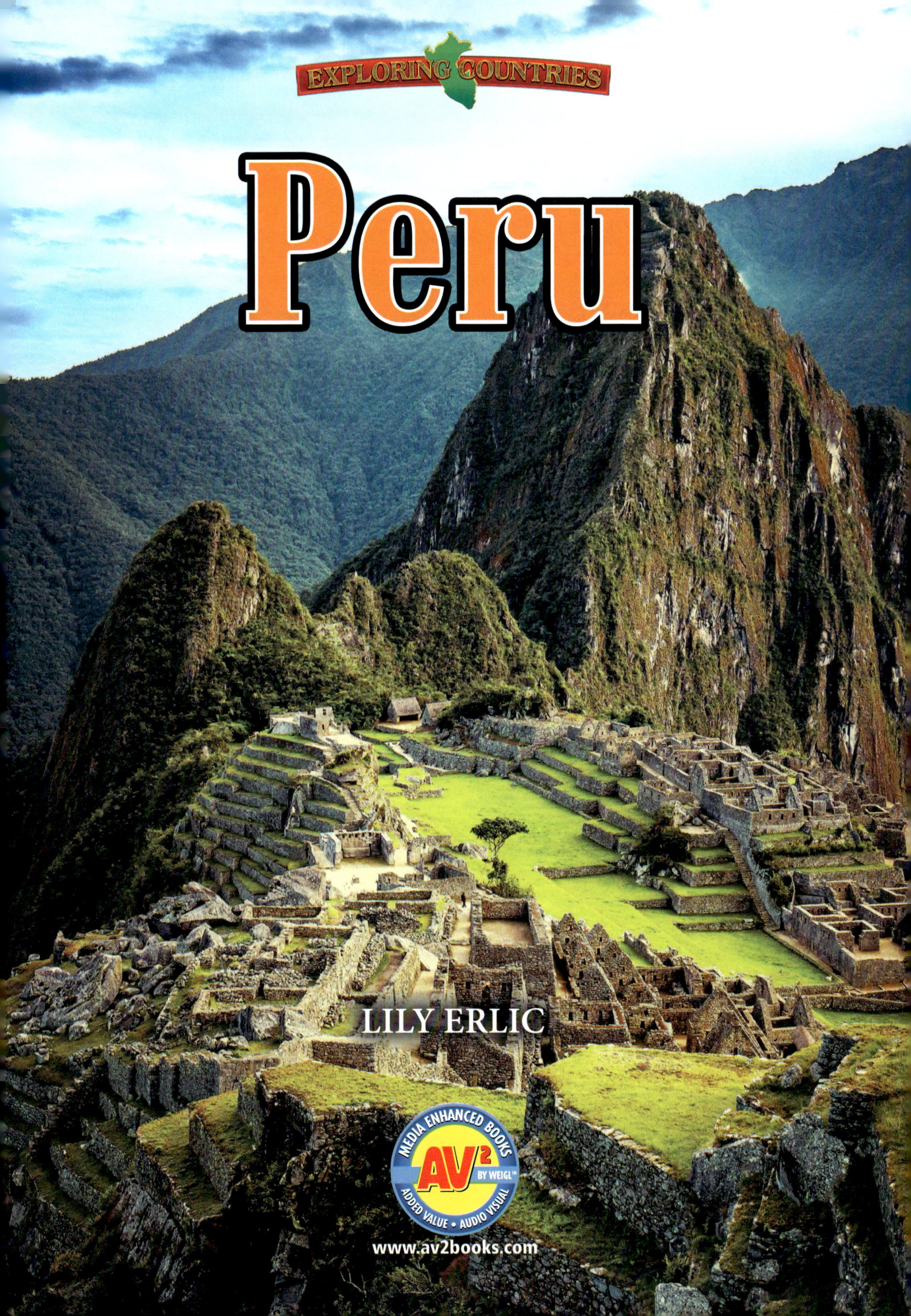
EXPLORING COUNTRIES
Peru
LILY ERLIC
MEDIA ENHANCED BOOKS
AV2
BY WEIGL
ADDED VALUE • AUDIO VISUAL
www.av2books.com

Go to www.av2books.com, and enter this book's unique code.

BOOK CODE

AVK93493

AV² by Weigl brings you media enhanced books that support active learning.

AV² provides enriched content that supplements and complements this book. Weigl's AV² books strive to create inspired learning and engage young minds in a total learning experience.

Your AV² Media Enhanced books come alive with...

Audio
Listen to sections of the book read aloud.

Video
Watch informative video clips.

Embedded Weblinks
Gain additional information for research.

Try This!
Complete activities and hands-on experiments.

Key Words
Study vocabulary, and complete a matching word activity.

Quizzes
Test your knowledge.

Slide Show
View images and captions, and prepare a presentation.

... and much, much more!

Published by AV² by Weigl
350 5th Avenue, 59th Floor
New York, NY 10118
Website: www.av2books.com

Library of Congress Cataloging-in-Publication Data

Names: Erlic, Lily, author.
Title: Peru / Lily Erlic.
Description: New York, NY : AV2 by Weigl, 2018. | Series: Exploring countries | Includes index. | Audience: Grade 4 to 6.
Identifiers: LCCN 2017055785 (print) | LCCN 2017056950 (ebook) | ISBN 9781489675132 (Multi User ebook) | ISBN 9781489675125 (hardcover : alk. paper) | ISBN 9781489680815 (softcover : alk. paper)
Subjects: LCSH: Peru--Juvenile literature.
Classification: LCC F3408.5 (ebook) | LCC F3408.5 .E75 2018 (print) | DDC 985--dc23
LC record available at https://lccn.loc.gov/2017055785

Printed in the United States of America in Brainerd, Minnesota
1 2 3 4 5 6 7 8 9 22 21 20 19 18

032019
120817

Project Coordinator Heather Kissock
Art Director Terry Paulhus

Photo Credits
Every reasonable effort has been made to trace ownership and to obtain permission to reprint copyright material. The publishers would be pleased to have any errors or omissions brought to their attention so that they may be corrected in subsequent printings.

Weigl acknowledges Getty Images, Newscom, iStock, and Alamy as its primary photo suppliers for this title.

Contents

AV² Book Code 2
Peru Overview 4
Exploring Peru 6
Land and Climate 8
Plants and Animals 10
Natural Resources 11
Tourism 12
Industry 14
Goods and Services 15
Indigenous Peoples 16
The Age of Exploration 17
Early Settlers 18
Population 20
Politics and Government 21
Cultural Groups 22
Arts and Entertainment 24
Sports 26
Mapping Peru 28
Quiz Time 30
Key Words 31
Index 31
Log on to www.av2books.com 32

Peru Overview

Peru is located in the western part of South America. It has a coastline on the Pacific Ocean and a varied landscape of mountains, rainforests, deserts, and beaches. Long ago, Peru was the center of the powerful **Inca Empire**. Peru was then a Spanish **colony**, until it became independent in the 1800s. Today, the country is growing its economy quickly. Many people visit Peru to tour the Amazon Rainforest. This region is home to many species, or types, of animals and plants. Tourists also visit the ruins of Machu Picchu, an ancient city built by the Inca in the year 1450.

Many Incan sites are found in the area called the Sacred Valley.

More than 1,800 bird species are found in Peru. Most live in the Amazon Rainforest.

Brightly colored craft items can be bought at markets throughout the country.

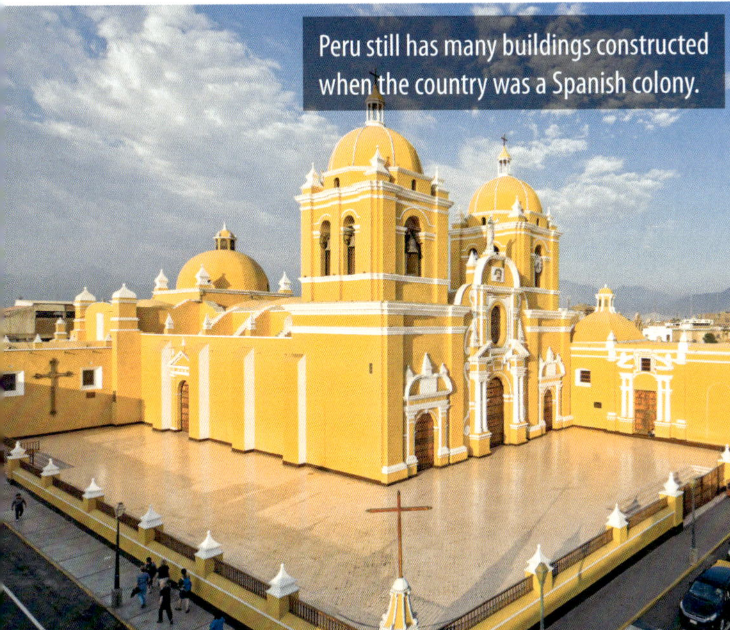
Peru still has many buildings constructed when the country was a Spanish colony.

There are about 7 million llamas in Peru, where they are used to produce wool, carry loads, and protect flocks of sheep.

Exploring Peru

Peru has an area of 496,225 square miles (1,285,216 square kilometers). The country is bordered by Chile and Bolivia on the south, Brazil on the east, and Colombia and Ecuador on the north. The Pacific Ocean forms Peru's western border. The Andes mountain range is located in western Peru. The Amazon Rainforest covers the eastern part of the country. Peru's major rivers include the Ucayali, which flows into the Amazon River, and the Marañón.

Mount Huascaran

Lima

Lake Titicaca

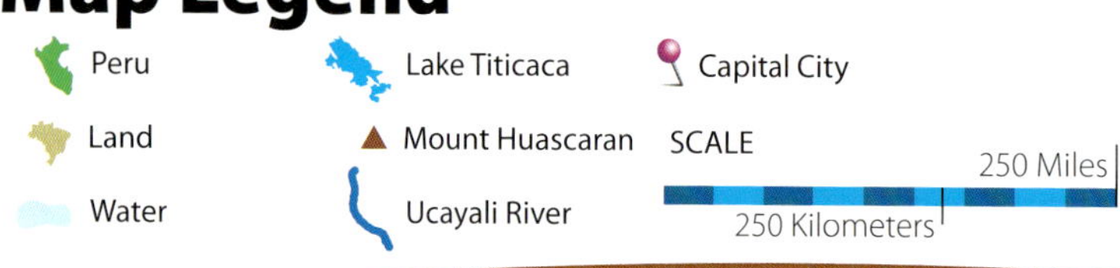

Mount Huascaran

Mount Huascaran is the highest peak in Peru. It is located in the Andes. The mountain has a height of 22,205 feet (6,768 meters).

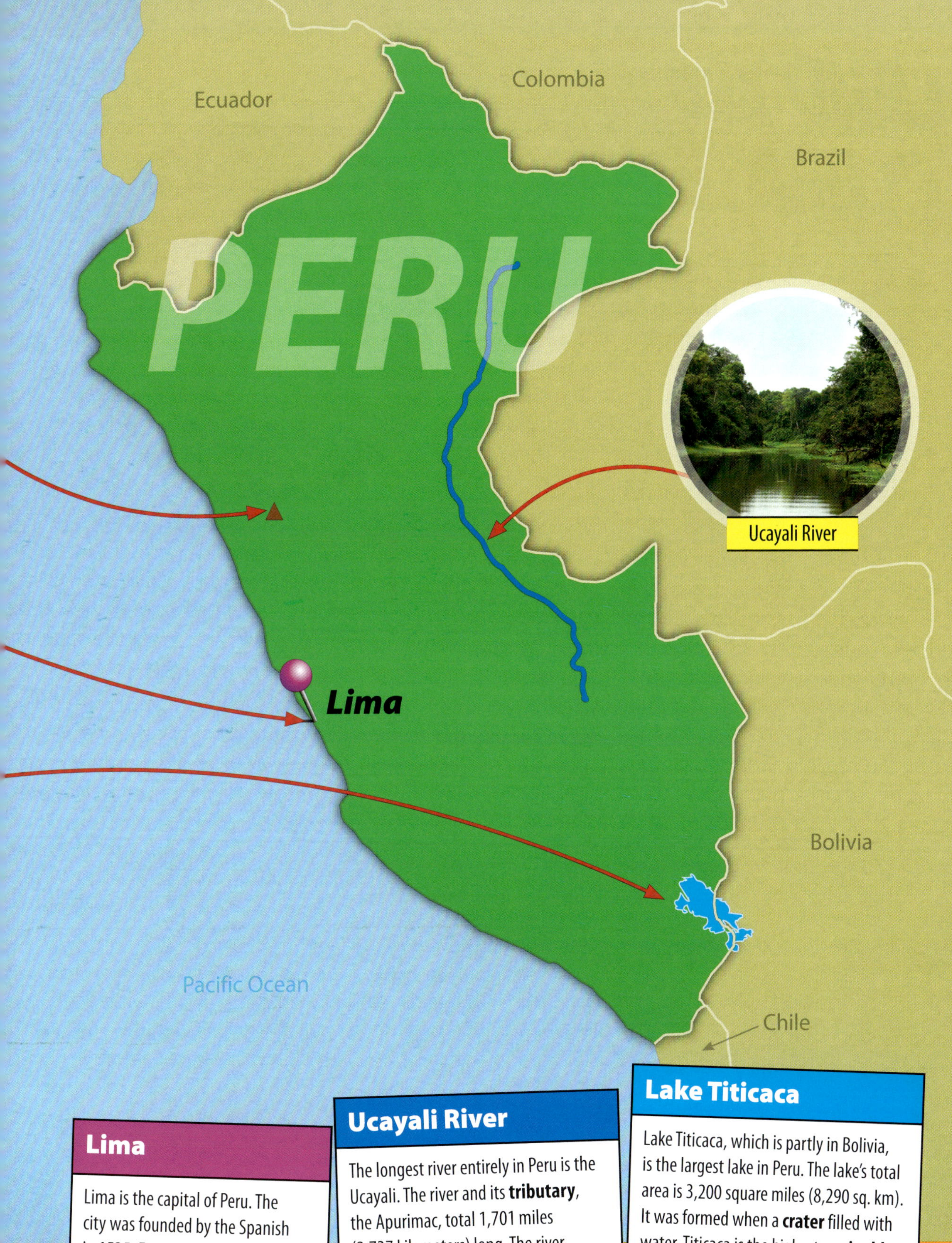

Lima

Lima is the capital of Peru. The city was founded by the Spanish in 1535. For many years, Lima was the capital of the Spanish empire in South America.

Ucayali River

The longest river entirely in Peru is the Ucayali. The river and its **tributary**, the Apurimac, total 1,701 miles (2,737 kilometers) long. The river begins in the east-central part of Peru and flows north.

Lake Titicaca

Lake Titicaca, which is partly in Bolivia, is the largest lake in Peru. The lake's total area is 3,200 square miles (8,290 sq. km). It was formed when a **crater** filled with water. Titicaca is the highest **navigable** lake in the world, at 12,500 feet (3,810 m) above sea level.

LAND AND CLIMATE

The Amazon River begins in the Andes Mountains of Peru and then flows across South America.

Peru is the third-largest country in South America. The Amazon Rainforest occupies about 60 percent of the country. The Andes, which run from north to south, also cover much of the land. Peru is situated along a fault, or boundary, between two **tectonic plates**. Sometimes, when plates slide past each other or collide, this activity causes earthquakes and volcanoes to occur in Peru.

Peru's three main geographic regions are the rainforest, the mountains, and the coastal area. The Amazon Rainforest is divided into two parts. The lowland jungle, or Selva Baja, is warm and humid. Temperatures reach as high as 100° Fahrenheit (38° Celsius). The highland jungle, or Selva Alta, has a milder climate. The greatest amount of rainfall in the rainforest occurs between November and March.

Rivers have cut deep canyons in the Vilcabamba mountains, which are part of the Andes, in south-central Peru.

The mountain area, or highlands, is called the Sierra. The Andes vary in height and steepness. The Central Andes are the highest and most rugged mountains in Peru. Many are often covered with snow, including the Cordillera Blanca. This portion of the Central Andes has some of the highest mountains in the world. In the Northern Andes, the mountains are lower, and their slopes are not steep. Much of the Southern Andes is a plateau, or an area of fairly flat land at high elevation above sea level.

A number of volcanoes are found in southwestern Peru, in an area known as the Valley of the Volcanoes. The country's highest **active** volcano is Nevado Coropuna. The most-active volcano is Ubinas, located east of Lake Titicaca.

Peru's coastal area, called the Costa, stretches along the Pacific shore. A narrow strip of land near the coast is a dry and sandy desert. The rest of the Costa is fairly dry as well. However, some areas receive enough rain so that crops and other plants can grow well. The weather tends to be cloudy and foggy during the colder months, which extend from May to November. Temperatures average about 53°F to 59°F (12°C to 15°C). In Peru's summer, from December to April, temperatures average about 77°F to 82°F (25°C to 28°C). More than 50 rivers that originate in the Andes run through the coastal region and into the Pacific Ocean.

Land and Climate BY THE NUMBERS

21,079 Feet
Elevation of the volcano Nevado Coropuna. (6,425 m)

13,000 Feet
Estimated height of the cloud of ash above the volcano Ubinas when it erupted in 2014. (3,960 m)

103 Inches Average amount of rainfall per year in the lowlands of the Peruvian rainforest. (2,616 millimeters)

PLANTS AND ANIMALS

A wide variety of plants and animals are found in Peru. There is great **biodiversity** because Peru contains many **ecosystems**. A number of species are found only in Peru.

One type of plant, *Puya raimondii,* also called the queen of the Andes, is the world's tallest flowering plant. It grows up to 30 feet (9 m) tall. Thousands of types of orchids are found in Peru, and new species are discovered each year.

The country's rainforest animals include the tamandua anteater. This creature lives in northern Peru, where it eats ants, bees, and other insects. Peru's rainforests are also home to bats, monkeys, sloths, and ocelots. Llamas and alpacas live in the highlands, and the South American fur seal and South American sea lion are found along the coast.

Bird species include the blackish oystercatcher and the Peruvian pelican. They both can be seen along the coast. Also found there is the Guanay cormorant, which has a bluish head and neck, with rings around its eyes.

Plants and Animals BY THE NUMBERS

More Than 6,000
Number of plant species in the Peruvian rainforest.

4.6 Million Acres
Area of the Manu **Biosphere** Reserve, created to protect the diverse plants and animals found in its highlands and rainforest. (1.8 million hectares)

About 3.5 Ounces
Weight of a pygmy marmoset, a type of monkey found in Peru's rainforest. (100 grams)

Humboldt penguins live in rocky areas along the Peruvian coast.

NATURAL RESOURCES

Peru's natural resources include a number of metals and minerals. Large amounts of gold, silver, and copper are mined. Other resources include iron ore, coal, lead, zinc, bismuth, manganese, phosphate, and potash.

Petroleum, or oil, and natural gas are also important resources in Peru. Many deposits of these resources have not yet been developed. Wood from the country's forests is another key resource. Cedar, oak, and mahogany are the main types of trees cut down for their lumber. Fertile soil, important for growing crops, is found in Peru's river valleys in the coastal region.

The Peru, or Humboldt, Current flows past Peru's coast. The water in this current is cool and low in salt, allowing many types of fish to thrive. Peruvian fishers catch large quantities of anchovies, sea bass, tuna, and swordfish.

Natural Resources BY THE NUMBERS

2.35 Million Tons
Total amount of copper produced in 2016 in Peru. (2.13 million metric tons)

3rd Peru's rank among world producers of silver, copper, and zinc.

10% Portion of the fish caught worldwide that comes from Peru.

Peru is the sixth-largest producer of gold in the world. About 165 tons (150 metric tons) are mined each year.

TOURISM

More than 3 million people from around the world visit Peru each year. Many come to tour the ruins of ancient sites. The most popular place is Machu Picchu, a **UNESCO** World Heritage Site in the Andes of southern Peru. The city was abandoned by the Inca in the 16th century, after the Spanish arrived in Peru. It was rediscovered in 1911.

Visitors to Lima can tour the San Francisco Church complex, originally constructed in 1557 and then rebuilt in the 17th century.

Cuzco, located about 50 miles (80 km) southeast of Machu Picchu, also began as an Incan city. It was taken over by Spanish settlers and remains a major city today. Notable sites in Cuzco include a cathedral built on top of an Incan palace, as well as other buildings from the time of Spanish colonization.

Another World Heritage Site is the center and oldest part of Lima. The city's main square includes buildings dating back to Spanish colonial times. Tourists can visit La Catedral, a cathedral that was damaged by earthquakes and rebuilt a number of times.

Tourists can explore the remains of Sacsayhuaman, a stone fortress built by the Inca near Cuzco.

North of Lima is the old city of Caral, also called Caral-Supe. It is thought to have been founded in 2600 BC. The main attractions are ancient monuments and six pyramids built around a courtyard. South of Lima are the **archaeological** sites of the Nazca and the Paracas peoples, who lived in the area before the Inca. Tourists also go on trips to Lake Titicaca's floating islands, which are made of reeds.

Arequipa, located between the highlands and the coast in southern Peru, is built on the side of a volcano. It is called the White City because many of its buildings were constructed using white rock created by volcanic eruptions. People often use Arequipa as a base for hiking and mountain climbing nearby. Hikers can descend into Colca Canyon, which is the second-deepest canyon in the world.

The Andes are also a popular destination. Train passengers can see spectacular views and Andean villages as they travel through the mountains. One well-known site in the Andes is the Ausangate Mountain, often called the Rainbow Mountain. It is striped with bright colors and looks as if it were painted with large brushstrokes.

Tourism BY THE NUMBERS

7,710 Feet Height of Machu Picchu above sea level. (2,350 m)

12 Number of UNESCO World Heritage Sites in Peru.

More than 450,000 Estimated number of visitors to Mistura, a food festival held in Lima each year.

11,155 Feet Depth of the Colca Canyon in southern Peru. (3,400 m)

Some tourists hike for several days to reach the Ausangate Mountain from Cuzco.

INDUSTRY

Peru's economy has improved in recent years, and its production of goods has increased. The country has been helped by loans and assistance from other nations and from international organizations. The government is trying to increase manufacturing in order to provide more jobs for people and reduce the number of Peruvians living in poverty.

Manufactured products include cement, glass, chemicals, and **textiles**. Fishing, mining, forestry, and agriculture are also major industries. Peru is among the world's leading producers of fishmeal, which is used as animal feed or as **fertilizer**. The country's principal agricultural products are sugarcane, cotton, rice, potatoes, corn, fruits, asparagus, soybeans, wheat, coffee, and quinoa.

Industries that manufacture products account for more than 16 percent of Peru's yearly **gross domestic product** (GDP). The mining industry makes up more than 14 percent of GDP. Farming, livestock-raising, and fishing account for about 7 percent.

Industry BY THE NUMBERS

$406 Billion Size of Peru's GDP in 2016.

17.4% Portion of workers in Peru with jobs in industries that produce goods, such as manufacturing and mining.

#1 Peru's rank among South American producers of potatoes.

In remote areas of Peru, logs can be transported only by riverboat.

GOODS AND SERVICES

More than one-half of all workers in Peru are employed in service industries. Rather than producing goods, workers in these industries provide services to other people. Service workers include hotel managers, tour guides, store clerks, and restaurant workers. Other examples of service workers are teachers, doctors, nurses, and housecleaners.

Peru trades with nations in many parts of the world. Peru **exports** the most goods to China, the United States, Switzerland, and Canada. Minerals and metals, coffee, vegetables, clothing, and textiles are among the products that Peru exports. The countries from which Peru **imports** the most goods are China, the United States, Brazil, and Mexico. Chemicals, plastics, electronics equipment, medicines, and some types of food are among the products that Peru imports.

Goods and Services BY THE NUMBERS

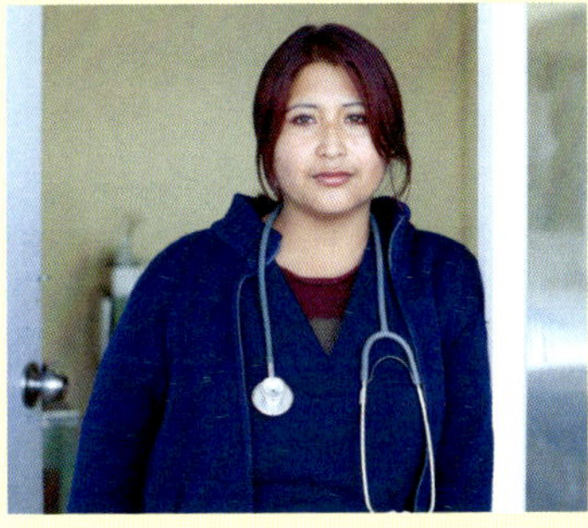

Almost 10 Million
Number of service workers in Peru.

2009 Year an agreement went into effect between the United States and Peru to increase trade.

About $37 Billion
Total value of Peru's yearly exports of goods.

More Than $35 Billion
Value of goods Peru imports each year.

Located on the Pacific Ocean, Callao is Peru's largest port and an important shipping center.

INDIGENOUS PEOPLES

People have lived in what is now Peru for thousands of years. The earliest peoples may have been in the area since about 20,000 BC. At first, these people were nomads. They traveled from place to place, hunting and gathering plants for food. Then, they began raising animals, such as llamas and alpacas, and they formed villages. People along the coast began fishing. The Chavín, Paracas, Moche, and Nazca were some of the early civilizations in the region.

In about AD 1200, the Inca arrived. Under their first emperor, Manco Capac, they set up their capital at Cuzco. The Inca fought with neighboring groups and conquered them. The Inca Empire had its center in Peru, but it extended north, into what is now Ecuador, and south, into present-day Bolivia, Chile, and Argentina.

The Inca spoke their own language, called Quechua. This language spread to peoples the Inca conquered. The Inca were skilled in architecture, or the design of buildings, and construction. They built lengthy roadways to connect parts of their empire. They created terraces, or step-like strips of flat land, on mountainsides to provide areas for farming. The Inca grew crops such as corn and potatoes, and they raised animals including llamas, alpacas, dogs, and guinea pigs.

Large line drawings, called Nazca Lines, were carved into the ground by Indigenous Peoples thousands of years ago. They can be seen clearly only from the air.

Indigenous Peoples BY THE NUMBERS

2900 BC Year ancient cultures in Peru began planting corn.

140 Million
Number of **adobe** blocks used by the Moche to build the Temple of the Sun near Trujillo in about AD 500.

THE AGE OF EXPLORATION

From the 15th to the 17th centuries, European explorers traveled by ship to other parts of the world to discover new trade routes and sources of wealth. In 1492, Christopher Columbus was sent by Spain across the Atlantic Ocean. He was trying to find a new sea route to Asia, but he came upon the Americas instead.

Beginning in about 1500, Spanish explorer Francisco Pizarro made a number of voyages to the Americas. He heard about the great wealth of the Inca Empire and received permission from the king of Spain to conquer it. Pizarro and his soldiers reached Peru in 1531 and set up a base camp. In November 1532, he led his forces to meet with the Incan emperor, Atahualpa, in the city of Cajamarca. Pizarro's soldiers attacked the Inca and captured Atahualpa. In 1533, Pizarro conquered Cuzco, which marked the end of the Inca Empire.

In the following years, battles took place between Spanish **conquistadors** and the Indigenous Peoples, until Spain controlled the entire region. There were also disputes between some of the Spaniards. In 1541, Pizarro died in a battle against soldiers loyal to another Spanish leader.

Atahualpa accepted Pizarro's invitation to meet in Cajamarca. The Incan leader was not afraid of Pizarro's small army.

The Age of Exploration BY THE NUMBERS

180 Number of men who traveled with Pizarro to Peru in 1531.

30,000 Estimated number of men in Atahualpa's army in 1532.

1533 Year Atahualpa was killed by the Spanish.

EARLY SETTLERS

After Spain took control of the region, settlers from that country arrived. They brought their language, customs, and traditions to Peru. Spanish settlers also brought the Roman Catholic religion to the area, and they built **monasteries** and churches. The Spanish forced the Indigenous Peoples to adopt their language and religion. They also brought people from Africa to work as slaves.

The Church of the Society of Jesus in Cuzco was built by the Spanish in the 1570s on the site of an Incan palace.

Some areas were divided into tracts, or large sections, of land under the *encomienda* system. This practice gave conquistadors or other Spaniards land to use, as well as power over the people living on the property. Many Spaniards forced the Indigenous Peoples to pay taxes and to work on farms or in mines, often without pay. In 1542, Spain passed the New Laws, which improved conditions somewhat for Peru's Indigenous Peoples.

During the colonial period, Lima was the center of government, culture, trade, and the court system.

In 1543, the king of Spain wanted more control over Spanish colonies in western South America. He established a **viceroyalty** there. Peru was the most valuable area under the viceroyalty. For many years, gold and silver from Peru were sent to Spain.

In the early 1800s, many colonists in South America wanted independence from Spanish rule. José de San Martín, a general who had led Argentina and Chile to independence, brought his forces to Peru and captured Lima. On July 28, 1821, San Martín proclaimed Peru's independence. He did not have enough forces to gain freedom for the highlands of Peru. San Martín asked for help from military leader Simón Bolívar. By 1824, Bolívar had won independence for all of Peru.

From 1879 to 1882, the War of the Pacific was fought by Peru and Bolivia against Chile. The dispute was over control of mineral-rich land. Chile won the war and gained land from Bolivia and Peru.

Thousands of Peruvians died during the War of the Pacific, which included many naval battles.

Early Settlers BY THE NUMBERS

1551 Year the National University of San Marcos, the oldest university in South America, was established in Lima.

2 Number of provinces Peru lost to Chile as a result of the War of the Pacific.

1854 Year slavery was abolished in Peru.

POPULATION

More than 31 million people live in Peru, and the country's population is growing by 1 percent each year. Peru's population density is 63 people per square mile (24 per sq. km). The population density in the United States is about 92 people per square mile (35 per sq. km).

More than three-fourths of Peruvians live in **urban** areas. About 10.2 million people live in the Lima **metropolitan area**. Arequipa, the second-largest city, is home to about 873,000 people.

The **median age** of Peruvians is about 28 years. This compares to 38 years in the United States. The population is young. More than 26 percent of Peruvians are under the age of 15, compared to about 19 percent in the United States. On average, Peruvians can expect to live to be about 74 years old, which is lower than the U.S. figure of 80.

Population BY THE NUMBERS

43rd Peru's rank by population size among the countries of the world.

About 827,000 Population of Trujillo, Peru's third-largest city.

94% Percentage of the people in Peru age 15 or older who can read.

Lima grew rapidly during the late 20th century, when many people moved there from the countryside.

POLITICS AND GOVERNMENT

The government of Peru is a presidential **republic**. There are three branches of government. They are the executive, legislative, and judicial branches.

The executive branch is headed by the president, who is elected for a five-year term. He or she appoints a cabinet, called the Council of Ministers. Members of the cabinet advise the president and head the departments of the government responsible for different activities, such as education or relations with other countries. The legislative branch consists of Congress, which has 130 members. Congress is responsible for passing the country's laws.

The judicial branch is made up of the country's courts. Judges on these courts are in charge of interpreting and applying the laws. The Supreme Court is the highest-level court in Peru.

Politics and Government BY THE NUMBERS

5 Years Length of the terms of office for members of Congress.

2016 Year that Pedro Pablo Kuczynski was elected president of Peru.

18 to 70 Ages during which voting is mandatory, or required, in Peru.

Congress meets at the Legislative Palace in Lima. Construction of the building began in 1904.

CULTURAL GROUPS

Thousands of Indigenous Peoples gather high in the Andes each year for the Snow Star Festival, or *Quoyllur Rit'i*.

Many groups contribute to Peru's culture. These groups include Indigenous Peoples, who are sometimes called Amerindians, the Spaniards who colonized Peru, and other settlers. Today, there are 51 Indigenous groups in Peru.

The Quechua, whose **ancestors** are the Inca, are the largest cultural group. They make up about 45 percent of the population. Mestizos, who are of mixed Amerindian and European ancestry, form 37 percent of the population. Europeans make up 15 percent. The rest of the population includes other Indigenous Peoples, as well as people of African or Asian ancestry.

Many Quechua and other Amerindian people, such as the Aymara, live in the southern Andes or in the Amazon. Some of these people still live the way their ancestors did. They shear the wool of llamas and alpacas to make yarn that is then used to produce clothing. They also make pottery, jewelry, and carvings, which they sell at local markets.

Quechuan people often wear handmade ponchos, which help them keep warm in the cool highlands of the Andes.

Spanish is Peru's official language. Quechua and Aymara have official status in the areas where they are spoken, and almost 50 other native languages are spoken in parts of Peru. More than 80 percent of the population is Roman Catholic. Some Peruvians practice a mix of Christian beliefs and traditional, indigenous faiths.

People in Peru's urban areas wear modern, Western-style clothing, but those in **rural** areas often wear traditional clothes. These often vary by community and region. In the Andes, textiles are used to make brightly colored ponchos, shirts, skirts, and belts. Hats are distinctive, varying by region. They are made in many different materials, colors, and styles.

Peruvians enjoy a variety of foods that reflect their diverse cultures and regions. Seafood is popular along the coast as well as in the Amazon, where the fish comes from the rivers. Seafood is so popular that the national dish is *ceviche*, which is raw fish prepared with lime juice, chilies, and onions. Asian influences are seen in dishes such as *lomo saltado*, which is beef cooked with potatoes, vegetables, chilies, and spices. In the north, roast goat, called *cabrito al horno*, is popular. In the highlands, people cook with potatoes, grains such as quinoa, and meat from llamas, chickens, and guinea pigs.

Cultural Groups BY THE NUMBERS

JUNE 24 Date on which Peruvians in Cuzco celebrate *Inti Raymi*, a festival honoring an Incan god.

84% Percentage of Peruvians who speak Spanish.

55 Number of types of corn grown in Peru, where it is used in many traditional dishes by different cultural groups.

Processions of ships are part of the Festival of St. Peter and St. Paul, celebrated by Catholic people each June.

ARTS AND ENTERTAINMENT

The Afro-Peruvian music of singer Susana Baca is popular in Peru and around the world.

Culture and the arts have been a part of Peruvian life for many centuries. Craft items created by ancient peoples can be seen in Lima at the Larco Museum and the National Museum of Archaeology, Anthropology, and History. Many aspects of art, music, and dance today reflect a mix of Indigenous, Spanish, and African influences.

Peruvians take part in festivals throughout the year. Every February, the city of Puno, near Lake Titicaca, holds the festival of the *Virgen de la Candelaria*, or Virgin of the Candles. People parade for miles through the streets as musicians play traditional songs.

Folk music in Peru is performed on a variety of instruments. They include flutes called *sikus* and *quenas*, **panpipes** called *zamponas*, and stringed instruments called *charangos*. Popular types of music include *huayno*, which developed in the Andes, and *criollo*, with Indigenous and Spanish elements.

Hundreds of teams of dancers compete at the festival of the *Virgen de la Candelaria*.

Peru has been home to many well-known painters. Diego Quispe Tito, who lived in the 1600s, was part of the Cuzco School of artists. These painters combined the styles of Indigenous artists and Spanish artists who arrived in Cuzco. Many of their works can be seen in Cuzco today. More recent artists include José Sabogal, Fernando de Szyszlo, and Víctor Delfín.

Lima has many museums presenting art from various time periods. They include the Lima Art Museum, with exhibits covering 3,000 years, and the National Museum of Peruvian Culture. The city also has numerous art galleries showing the work of modern Peruvian artists.

One of Peru's best-known writers is Mario Vargas Llosa, who was born in Arequipa in 1931. His novels include *The Time of the Hero* and *Aunt Julia and the Scriptwriter*. Vargas Llosa's works are often based on his life and problems in current Peruvian society. They have been translated into many languages and are read around the world.

Arts and Entertainment BY THE NUMBERS

10 HOURS Length of the *danza de tijeras*, or scissors dance, performed by men from villages in the Andes.

2010 Year Mario Vargas Llosa won the Nobel Prize in Literature, awarded for outstanding achievement.

More Than 19 Million Number of times Peruvian singer Wendy Sulca's most-popular video has been viewed on YouTube.

Intihuatana, a large sculpture by Fernando de Szyszlo, is located in a park in Lima. Szyszlo, also known for his modern paintings, died in October 2017.

SPORTS

Soccer, called football in Peru, is the country's most popular sport. The men's and women's national teams represent Peru in international competition. The men's team has played in the **FIFA** World Cup, the highest-level international tournament, in 1930, 1970, 1978, and 1982. In November 2017, the Peruvians defeated a team from New Zealand to qualify for the 2018 World Cup.

In past years, Teofiló Cubillas was one of Peru's best soccer players. In 1975, he helped his team win the Copa América tournament. This event determines South America's championship team.

Vanessa Palacios has played on the national volleyball team since 2005.

Volleyball is another popular sport in Peru. The women's national volleyball team won a silver medal at the 1988 Olympic Games in Seoul, South Korea. Natalia Málaga was a well-known volleyball player who played on that team. She was also on the teams that won a silver medal at the Pan American Games in 1987, as well as bronze medals in 1983 and 1991.

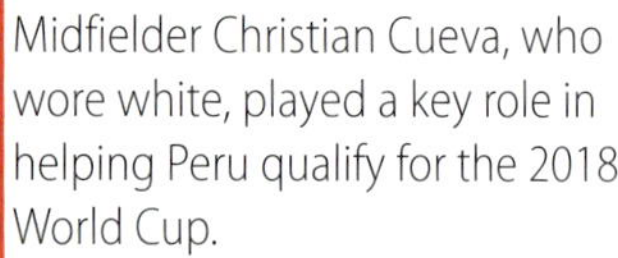

Midfielder Christian Cueva, who wore white, played a key role in helping Peru qualify for the 2018 World Cup.

Cecilia Tait was another star volleyball player for Peru. She was the captain of the 1988 Olympic team. After her retirement as a player, she served in Peru's Congress.

Peru has participated in the Summer Olympic Games many times, winning four medals. Edwin Vásquez won a gold medal in shooting in 1948. Peruvian athletes won silver medals in shooting events in 1984 and 1992, as well as the volleyball silver medal in 1988. Peru participated in the Winter Games in 2010 and 2014.

Both residents and tourists enjoy surfing along Peru's Pacific coast. The country has also produced some notable professional surfers. In 1965, when he was 22 years old, Felipe Pomar won the men's world championship in surfing. He was the first Peruvian to win the title. Sofía Mulánovich won the women's title in 2004.

Spectators have enjoyed watching bullfighting in Peru since the 16th century, when Pizarro organized the first such event in Lima. Bullfights take place in Lima from October to December. A festival known as the *Feria Taurina del Senor de los Milagros*, or Fair of the Lord of Miracles, marks the beginning of the season.

Sports BY THE NUMBERS

1959 Year Alex Olmedo, who was born in Peru, won the men's singles title at the Wimbledon tennis tournament.

17 Years Old Age of Ariana Orrego in 2016 when she became the first athlete to represent Peru in gymnastics at the Olympics.

MORE THAN 12 FEET Average height of the waves at Pico Alto beach in Punta Hermosa, Peru. (3.7 m)

Sofía Mulánovich was named to the Surfers Hall of Fame in 2007, becoming the first person from South America to receive the honor.

Mapping Peru

We use many tools to interpret maps and to understand locations of features such as cities, states, lakes, and rivers. The map below has many tools to help interpret information on the map of Peru.

MAP LEGEND

- Capital City
- City
- Body of Water
- River
- Country Border
- Mountain
- Longitude & Latitude
- Peru
- Other Countries

N E S W

SCALE

0 — 175 Miles

0 — 175 Kilometers

Mapping Tools

- The compass rose shows north, south, east, and west. The points in-between represent northeast, northwest, southeast, and southwest.
- The map scale shows that the distances on a map represent much longer distances in real life. If you measure the distance between objects on a map, you can use the map scale to calculate the actual distance in miles or kilometers between those two points.
- The lines of latitude and longitude are long lines that appear on maps. The lines of latitude run east to west and measure how far north or south of the equator a place is located. The lines of longitude run north to south and measure how far east or west of the Prime Meridian a place is located. A location on a map can be found by using two numbers where latitude and longitude meet. This number is called a coordinate and is written using degrees and direction. For example, the city of Lima would be found at 12°S and 77°W on a map.

Map It!

Using the map and the appropriate tools, complete the activities below.

Locating with latitude and longitude

1. What city is located at 13.5°S and 72°W?
2. What mountain is located at 9°S and 77.6°W?
3. What lake is located at 15.9°S and 69.3°W?

Distances between points

4. Using the map scale and a ruler, calculate the approximate distance between the cities of Lima and Cuzco.
5. Using the map scale and a ruler, calculate the approximate distance between Lima and Puno.
6. Using the map scale and a ruler, calculate the approximate distance between Puno and Arequipa.

ANSWERS 1. Cuzco 2. Mount Huascaran 3. Lake Titicaca 4. 350 miles (560 km) 5. 525 miles (845 km) 6. 175 miles (280 km)

Quiz Time

Test your knowledge of Peru by answering these questions.

1 What is the capital of Peru?

2 What are the three main geographic regions in Peru?

3 What is the highest active volcano in Peru?

4 In what city is the Larco Museum located?

5 What is Peru's national dish?

6 How many Indigenous groups live in Peru today?

7 In what year did José de San Martín proclaim Peru's independence from Spain?

8 What group of people built the city of Machu Picchu?

9 What portion of Peru's population is Roman Catholic?

10 What is Peru's most popular sport?

ANSWERS

1. Lima
2. The rainforest, the mountains, and the coastal area
3. Nevado Coropuna
4. Lima
5. *Ceviche*
6. 51
7. 1821
8. The Inca
9. More than 80 percent
10. Soccer

Key Words

active: referring to a volcano that has erupted in recent times
adobe: bricks or materials for building made of sun-dried earth and straw
ancestors: people in one's family or cultural groups who lived in past times
archaeological: related to the study of human history, often by examining objects
biodiversity: the number and variety of species in a geographic region
biosphere: living things and the environment in which they live
colony: an area or country that is under the control of another country
conquistadors: military leaders during Spain's conquest of parts of the Americas during the 16th century
crater: a bowl-shaped low area of land
ecosystems: communities of living things and resources
exports: sells goods to other countries
fertilizer: a substance used to improve soil and help plants grow
FIFA: the Fédération Internationale de Football Association, which sets the rules for international soccer and organizes international tournaments
gross domestic product: the total value of the goods and services a country or area produces
imports: buys goods from other countries
Inca Empire: a region covering much of western South America that was ruled by the Inca native peoples during the 1400s and early 1500s
median age: the age that half the people in a population are younger than and half are older than
metropolitan area: a major city and the built-up areas around it
monasteries: places where monks, or men in a religious order, live and work
navigable: referring to a body of water that can be used by ships
panpipes: wind instruments consisting of pipes of different lengths tied together in a row
republic: a form of government in which the head of state is elected
rural: relating to the countryside
tectonic plates: sections of Earth's surface that move very slowly
textiles: cloth and yarn or thread used to make cloth
tributary: a river that flows into a larger river
UNESCO: the United Nations Educational, Scientific, and Cultural Organization, whose main goals are to promote world peace and eliminate poverty through education, science, and culture
urban: relating to cities and towns
viceroyalty: a region governed by a representative, called a viceroy, of a king or queen

Index

agriculture 14, 16
Amazon Rainforest and River 4, 5, 6, 8, 22, 23
Amerindians 22
Andes Mountains 6, 8, 9, 12, 13, 22, 23, 25
animals 5, 10, 16
Arequipa 13, 20, 25
art 24, 25
Aymara 22, 23

Baca, Susana 24
biodiversity 10
birds 5, 10
Bolívar, Simón 19
Bolivia 6, 7, 16, 19
borders 6

Chile 6, 7, 16, 19
climate 8, 9
coastal region 9, 10, 11, 23
colonial period 12, 18, 19
Cuzco 12, 13, 16, 17, 18, 23, 25

dance 24, 25

economy 14, 15
encomienda system 18
exports 15

gross domestic product 14

imports 15
Inca Empire 4, 12, 16, 17
Indigenous Peoples 16, 17, 18, 22

lakes 7
languages 16, 23
Lima 7, 12, 13, 18, 19, 20, 21, 24, 25, 27
llamas 5, 10, 16, 22

Machu Picchu 4, 12, 13
manufacturing 14
mestizos 22
minerals and mining 11, 14, 15
music 24, 25

natural resources 11

oil 11
Olympics 26, 27

Pizarro, Francisco 17
plants 10
population 20, 22

Quechua 16, 22, 23

rainforest 4, 5, 6, 8, 10
rivers 6, 7, 8, 9

San Martín, José de 19
service industries 15
soccer 26
Spain 4, 5, 7, 12, 17, 18, 19, 22
Sulca, Wendy 25
Szyszlo, Fernando de 25

Titicaca, Lake 7, 9, 13, 24
tourism 12, 13

Vargas Llosa, Mario 25
viceroyalty 19
volcanoes 8, 9, 13
volleyball 26, 27

War of the Pacific 19

Log on to www.av2books.com

AV² by Weigl brings you media enhanced books that support active learning. Go to www.av2books.com, and enter the special code found on page 2 of this book. You will gain access to enriched and enhanced content that supplements and complements this book. Content includes video, audio, weblinks, quizzes, a slide show, and activities.

AV² Online Navigation

Audio
Listen to sections of the book read aloud.

Book Pages
AV² pages directly correspond to pages in the book.

Video
Watch informative video clips.

Embedded Weblinks
Gain additional information for research.

Key Words
Study vocabulary, and complete a matching word activity.

Try This!
Complete activities and hands-on experiments.

Quizzes
Test your knowledge.

Slide Show
View images and captions, and prepare a presentation.

AV² was built to bridge the gap between print and digital. We encourage you to tell us what you like and what you want to see in the future.

Sign up to be an AV² Ambassador at www.av2books.com/ambassador.

Due to the dynamic nature of the Internet, some of the URLs and activities provided as part of AV² by Weigl may have changed or ceased to exist. AV² by Weigl accepts no responsibility for any such changes. All media enhanced books are regularly monitored to update addresses and sites in a timely manner. Contact AV² by Weigl at 1-866-649-3445 or av2books@weigl.com with any questions, comments, or feedback.